This book is dedicated to my nephews, Noah and Jordan Potash,
and to Hayley Green.

Special Thanks to Mark Green

Doodles the Dodo

Written and Illustrated by

Wendy Wyman Campbell

Once upon a time, a long time ago, there lived the most silly looking, most lovable, most trusting birds in the world. They were called Dodos. The most charming, most famous Dodo that ever lived was named Doodles. Doodles and his family, along with the other Dodos, lived on the beautiful tropical island called Mauritius.

Mauritius was, and still is, such a beautiful place. It was like being in heaven! It was so peaceful and so easy to live happily without fear. Delicious fruits fell onto the ground, and lay waiting to be eaten. Everything was so easy, and beautiful! None of the Dodos ever felt a need to leave their beautiful island home. They were happy just where they were.

Doodles loved it when his parents would tell him stories at bedtime, especially the story of how his great, great, great, great, great, great, great grandparents flew over to Mauritius from a far away land called Africa, a long time ago.

Over time, and many generations, Mama Dodo explained that the Dodos' wings became smaller and smaller since there was really no need to fly. And the Dodos' legs got shorter and shorter since there was no need to have long legs to run from enemies. There were no enemies! No need to have a long neck either. The food was right on the ground and easy to pick up. It was so warm, that their feathers got lighter and fluffier. And their bodies got rounder and rounder. "And that is why we Dodos look the way we do today!" was how Mama Dodo always ended the story. Then she would kiss him good-night and tuck him in.

Doodles loved to dream about what it would be like to have wings. Why, if he had wings, he could visit faraway lands and make new friends. He already knew everyone on the island, because he was very friendly and outgoing. He was a little celebrity because of not only his charisma, but also because of his rainbow-colored tail feathers and wings. Everyone else had yellow tail feathers and wings.

No one could resist Doodles when he turned on his charm, with his dazzling eyes, and his happy smile. Doodles had many friends and loved to find new friends to share adventures with. He liked to make friends with everyone he met on the island. He knew all the other birds, the butterflies, the snails, the crabs, the frogs, the monkeys, and the iguanas.

Wherever Doodles went, he was greeted with a smile, and "Hi, Doodles!" and "How's it going, Doodles?" and "Have a great day, Doodles!" Life was so sweet. BUT life was getting a little boring for Doodles. His heart yearned for a great adventure.

One day, while Doodles was on the beach playing in the surf, he looked up and saw a very strange thing in the distant horizon. It was coming closer and closer. Doodles had never, ever seen anything like it before, so he didn't know that it was called a ship. It was a ship full of strange creatures. At least they seemed strange to Doodles, since he never saw anything like them before!

He was very curious and eager to make new friends. Maybe he could take a ride on their ship! Maybe he could see faraway lands! Maybe he could make new friends! Doodles flapped his little wings in excitement, and called out, "HI!!!"

"Hellooo!! My name is Doodles! Doodles the Dodo! What is your name? Hiiii!!!"
He looked so cute and made so much noise that one of the creatures came over to
him and talked to him. "Hi, there, Doodles. So nice to meet you. My name is Lady
Lulu. I am the wife of Captain Courage. What a beautiful island you live on!"

"Wow!" said Doodles. "I have never met anyone like you before! What is that and
what are those?" Doodles asked excitedly, as he pointed.

"I have never met anyone like you either," Lady Lulu replied. "That is called a ship.
We came all the way from a faraway land called England, and those are people and
our farm animals – we have brought with us goats and pigs and cats and dogs.

Doodles already liked Lady Lulu very much. He felt sad to have to lose a new friend so soon. Then he had a great idea. "Lady Lulu, I was wondering, would it be OK with you if I came with you on the sh-sh-sh-shi…"

"Ship," Lady Lulu kindly helped him with this new word.

"Yes, ship. I want to go on the ship with you to faraway lands and have great adventures and make new friends!" Doodles was so excited at the thought of this idea, he could hardly stand still and jumped up and down with joy.

"Well, Doodles, you will need to ask your mother and father first, and I would like to meet them. If it's OK with them, then, yes, Doodles, you are welcome to come with us to England as my special guest."

"YAY!!!!" Doodles exclaimed and jumped up and down. "Thank you, Lady Lulu, thank you! This is what I have been waiting for!" Lady Lulu smiled and affectionately patted Doodles on the head. "I will take good care of you, Doodles. I promise."

Doodles' mother and father gave him permission to go on his grand adventure since they knew how much it meant to him. Tears fell from their eyes as Doodles kissed them good-bye. "We will miss you so much, Doodles. Please always remember that we love you!" said his mother. "Yes, son, and remember this is your home. We will always be here for you," said his father.

Doodles cried a few tears himself, because he knew he would miss his parents very much. Then he had to hurry and get on the boat since everyone was waiting for him. Lady Lulu put her arm around Doodles and they both waved goodbye to Doodles' parents and all his friends on the beach. All his family and friends were there to wish him luck on his exciting journey! Although he knew he would miss everyone, he also felt very excited about his grand adventure ahead.

The days were spent singing and laughing and making merry. The ocean was HUGE and there were some days when they saw nothing but ocean and sky. Doodles entertained everyone with his singing, "Doo doo doo, dee dah dah dah, here we go, so far, far, far! Doo doo doo, dah dee dee dee, in the middle of the sea, sea, sea!" and so on and so forth.

Friendly whales came close to the boat with their baby whales out of curiosity and waved hello. Dolphins also came and swam quickly by the boat, and did acrobatics to entertain everyone. Even sea turtles popped by to poke their heads up and say hello and wave. Doodles was having so much fun! It was beyond his wildest dreams!

Just when Doodles was starting to feel bored on the ship, there was sight of land. It was England! Doodles asked Lady Lulu to tell him about England. Lady Lulu smiled and said, "Doodles, you are going to be treated like royalty in England. I am going to introduce you to my cousin, the Queen of England, as my very special friend. We will have tea at her beautiful castle and you will meet new friends like the Queen's peacocks. Have you ever met a peacock before, Doodles?" Doodles just shook his head no, feeling too excited to say anything at all. He felt like the luckiest Dodo in the world. He wanted to write a letter to his mom and dad to tell them all about his trip as soon as he got a chance.

Soon, they boarded off the ship and they were met by lots of friendly people. Doodles and Lady Lulu got into a gilded carriage and headed for the Queen's castle.

Inside the castle, Doodles was amazed at the splendor of this new place. Lady Lulu and Doodles were introduced to the Queen and they proceeded to have a lovely teatime. One of the Queen's beautiful peacocks joined them as well. "Doodles, it is such a delightful pleasure to meet you!" said the Queen, smiling fondly at Doodles. "Thank you, Your Majesty, and I am so honored to be able to have tea with you here today." Lady Lulu smiled approvingly at Doodles. Doodles' famous charm was working on the Queen, too. Wherever Doodles went, everyone seemed to love him!

So Doodles spent his days playing croquet with the peacocks, having teatime with his many new friends, eating at lavish banquets, taking naps whenever he felt like it, and generally having a grand old time.

One day, Lady Lulu got a letter from Captain Courage that made her cry. Unfortunately, the sailors thought that Dodos were just a kind of turkey and ate them all! Now Doodles the Dodo had no family. Now Doodles the Dodo was the one and only Dodo in the whole world! Lady Lulu knew that Doodles would be very, very sad to hear this news, but she would have to tell him. He had already asked her why there were no letters from his parents. She did not want to tell him this horrible news, but she knew she had to.

The next day, Lady Lulu took Doodles for a walk in the garden.

"Doodles, I'm sorry to say that I have some very bad news for you," said Lady Lulu. A tear started to fall out of the corner of her eye, and that made Doodles get a tear in his eye as well. "Your mother and father are not in this world anymore, but at least they are in Heaven where they are very happy, I am sure."

Doodles was shocked! At first, he could not say anything. Then he said, "Why? Why did they go to Heaven?" Lady Lulu just said, "Some things seem to have no reason. You just have to accept it, and live your life as best as you can. Someday in the future, you will see them in Heaven, when it is your time." Lady Lulu put her arms around Doodles and they both cried until there were no more tears. Doodles really missed his mother and father very much.

Lady Lulu did everything she could do to try to make sure that Doodles had everything he needed and wanted. But ever since that day, Doodles never felt as happy as he did before and he often felt very, very sad.

To cheer Doodles up, Lady Lulu decided to have a big party for him, and sent invitations to all his new friends.

It was a wonderful party! All his friends came to join in the fun. They had lots of cake and ice cream. Even the Queen made a grand entrance and brought in a special present just for him.

"Doodles, you have been such a wonderful and lovable friend, and Lady Lulu and I want to give you this special gift. Go ahead, untie the bow!"

Doodles untied the big red bow, and he was amazed to see a statue of himself! "Wow!" Doodles exclaimed. "He looks just like me!" He felt so flattered and it was good to see another Dodo finally, even if it was just a statue and couldn't talk or play games. He could make pretend anyway! "Thank you soooo much!" Doodles said to Lady Lulu and the Queen. Everyone gave Doodles a hug and a kiss. For the first time in a long time, Doodles felt happy again.

The Queen said, "Doodles, I am going to make this day a special holiday in your honor and your parents and for all the Dodos who ever lived on this earth. From now on, the first day of Spring shall be called "Remember the Dodos Day" and the Dodo will always, always be remembered! Long live the Dodo!"

"Long live the Dodo!" chimed in everyone together, and Doodles felt
so happy he started singing a song "DoDoDo, Da Doo Doo Doo,
That's all I want to say to you! DoDoDo Da Dee Dee Dee, long live the
Dodo in your memory!!!" And everyone in London gathered to show
Doodles that they loved him and the Dodos will never, ever be forgotten!

Many, many years later, the statue of Doodles the Dodo is now in a beautiful park for everyone to enjoy. Most importantly, almost everyone knows about how the wonderful Dodos once walked on this planet, but now there are none. Everyone must be careful to make sure that no more wonderful creatures disappear from this earth like the fantastic bird known as the Dodo.

Some thoughts for you...

Did you know that the Dodos were first discovered by Dutch sailors in 1589 AD? The last Dodo died in 1681, since many of them were not only eaten by the sailors but their habitat was forever changed by the sailors and the animals they brought with them such as pigs, goats, cats and dogs.

It's a lesson about how fragile life on this planet is!

Did you know that the Dodo was a relative of the pigeon family?

At least we have plenty of pigeons to remind us of the fabulous Dodo!

One thing you can do to help preserve life on this planet is to always throw your trash in a trash bin. Never leave litter! Also, when you travel in a national park, never take plants or feed the animals.

Can you think of some other ways to help preserve the animals?